IT'S A WONDERFUL WIFE

A novella

CAMILLE PAGÁN

OTHER BOOKS BY
CAMILLE PAGÁN

Everything Must Go
Don't Make Me Turn This Life Around
This Won't End Well
I'm Fine and Neither Are You
Woman Last Seen in Her Thirties
Forever Is the Worst Long Time
Life and Other Near-Death Experiences
The Art of Forgetting

Visit CamillePagan.com/subscribe
to be the first to find out about her
new books, giveaways, and updates.

Text copyright © 2021 by Camille Pagán

Published by Even Better Co., Ann Arbor, MI

www.camillepagan.com

Cover design and illustration by EBookLaunch.com

ISBN: 979-8-9851702-2-1

ONE

"No man is a failure who has friends."
—Clarence the Angel, *It's a Wonderful Life*

"Bailey? I've got bad news." My Aunt Billie stared at me like she was about to tell me the Grinch had just made off with all of our Christmas presents.

I glanced up from the pile of papers on my desk. "Can it wait just a few? I'm wrapping up payroll."

She grimaced. "Yeah, that's the thing. I, uh. I . . . lost some money."

"Lost? What do you mean, 'lost'?" I leaned forward to sniff for whiskey and regret. Like me, Billie didn't handle the holidays too well. Because while everyone else was fa-la-la-ing about the most wonderful time of the year, we were forced to plaster on eggnog-guzzling grins and pretend it wasn't the anniversary of my parents' death. I was just twenty when my mom, who was Billie's sister, asked my dad to take her out on a drive on a snowy Christmas Eve. I'll never know exactly what happened, but I told my younger sister, Harriet, whom we'd always called Hattie, that they were singing carols to each other when they hit a patch of ice. In that version of the story, they didn't have time to realize they were careening directly into a Douglas fir—you know, the kind you might decorate with twinkle lights and ornaments, if it wasn't busy killing you. Eighteen years later and I still can't shake the blues when December rolls around.

"Well, you know how the cannery isn't doing so hot?" Billie's hands were balled into fists and her face, which was lined as much with sadness as age, was all twisted up.

"Of course." My parents had owned the canning factory that employed half of the people in our small town in upstate New York. After they died, I left Cornell in the middle of my sophomore year to take care of Hattie and learn everything I never wanted to know about food production. "But we have a plan in place to turn things around. Remember?" Unfortunately, I didn't know if said plan—which involved leasing out half our space to a liquor distillery—would work, as we had yet to find a spirits company interested in renting from us. But hope sprang eternal, or so I was told.

"Um. I . . ." She glanced out the one window in my closet-sized office, which looked out on the production line instead of the river next to the cannery. I preferred the view of dozens of people in hairnets and aprons putting beans in tin cans, over and over and over. Picturesque it was not— but I was a stickler about safety, and there was something deeply comforting in knowing that every single person George's Cannery employed would leave with a fair day's wage and all their digits intact.

"Billie, just tell me. I can handle it."

She turned back to me, then flung herself into the chair on the other side of my desk, threw her arm over her eyes, and began to cry. My aunt had always been too entrenched in her permanent adolescence to be much of a surrogate parent to me. Then again, she didn't have to be. Not when I was the stand-in parent for everyone except for the children that my husband, Chris, and I couldn't manage to have.

"Oh, Bailey, I'm so sorry. I was just trying to pull us out of the mess we're in and I went and did the exact opposite. I mean, Judd said his guy was the very best and that he'd made a mint in New York. He swore we'd see huge returns in a month, and even bigger ones after the new year. Now he won't answer my texts. And when I called the number to his office, it turned out to be a temp agency."

Judd was my aunt's high school flame, and he was as trustworthy as an underfed snake. This was way worse than I'd thought.

I took a deep breath, trying to stay calm. "How much money are we talking about, exactly?"

Her voice was barely a whisper. "Two hundred thousand."

Do not vomit, I ordered myself. *Do* not *vomit.* "You're saying the money came out of the company's bank account." This was not so much a question as a statement; I already knew the answer. And I knew we were screwed. Why hadn't the bank alerted me that Billie had made such a massive transaction? Technically she was on the account because she was the VP. Still. We were a lean operation—and by lean, I mean we were barely turning enough profit to pay our employees twice a month. I did some quick mental math and determined we had another three hundred fifty thousand left, which was half of what we needed to cover the winter property taxes, insurance, and nearly two hundred paychecks. Worse, the next payment from the agricultural giant who was our main client wouldn't arrive until mid-January. Something told me the Keebler elves weren't going to pick up the phone when I called to see if they'd make the deposit two weeks early.

"Bailey, I really am so sorry. Please forgive me."

"It's okay, Billie." She had been loyal and loving to me all these years, and she was my closest connection to my mom. The last thing I was going to do was pour salt on her wounds. "Don't worry another minute. I'll handle it."

Her face was drawn. "How?"

How? *How?* My mind was as blank as the day I showed up on the factory floor after my parents died. I was a twenty-year-old college dropout with absolutely no understanding of supply chains, food production, or, you know, how to run a business. I remember looking out at the two hundred and three people that my parents employed, every single one of whom was staring at me with pity. Not only because my parents had died, but because they didn't think I could do the job.

Well, I'd shown them—or so I thought. But all these years later, it turned out they were right.

I forced my face into my best "It's going to be fine" smile and gave Billie a hug. But deep down, I knew getting out of this would require a Christmas miracle.

TWO

My mom loved Christmas. Like, *really* loved it. She had
a hard-and-fast rule about not decorating until after
Thanksgiving, but as soon as everyone else had stuffed
themselves into a turkey and pumpkin pie coma, she'd drag
the boxes of lights and garlands out of the attic. The next
morning, we'd rise early, bundle up, and drive out to the
Christmas tree farm. There, Hattie and I would grumble
about the cold while she and my father strode through row
after row of pines, searching for the perfect tree—which
always did turn out to be perfect, even if was never quite
large enough for all the ornaments my mom had amassed
over the years.

The big event, however, was her annual Christmas
party. Everyone was invited: friends, relatives, neighbors,
cannery employees, and basically anyone else who didn't
have somewhere to be. People piled into our small home
to sing carols and played my mom's famous white elephant

game and left feeling like all was right in the world.

It really *was* the most wonderful time of the year. Hattie and I were never too old or too cool to come flying down the stairs to see what had been left in our stockings and under the tree for us, or to cuddle on the sofa with our parents to watch *It's a Wonderful Life* yet again. We never cared that we woke up on December 26 to a house that looked like it had been looted by a bunch of angry elves. All that prep work and then all that cleaning, even the inevitable letdown that set in not long after the ball dropped in Times Square a week later—it was worth the joy the holidays brought us.

I never felt like that again after my parents died. But every year, Chris and I hosted a holiday party, just like my parents had always done—only on Christmas Eve, rather than Christmas Day. As painful as it was to celebrate the worst day of my life, the party was the best way I could think of to honor their memory.

But how could I throw it this year, knowing that nearly every person attending was about to discover I'd ruined their life? I was imagining the confusion and anger my employees would feel when they realized I'd invited them into my home only to leave them high and dry when Jessalyn stuck her head into my office.

"You ready for the holidays, Bailey?"

As was our tradition, the cannery shut down at three on the day before Christmas Eve and reopened the day after the New Year; I'd just announced over the loudspeaker that it was time to close up shop, and everyone was marching into the locker rooms. Jessalyn had been at the cannery longer than anyone else and had known me since I was in diapers.

"Mostly." I tried to smile, but my lips refused to curve.

"You okay?" Her large brown eyes were kind but curious. "Child, forgive me, but you don't look quite right."

"I'm going to be fine." *Just as soon as I figure out how to pay you*, I thought. We'd handed out holiday bonuses at the beginning of the month, thank goodness, but everyone's direct deposit was due the day after Christmas. Would I give them half? Pay some workers but not others? I would have dipped into my own savings, except that was . . . virtually nonexistent, to be honest. My salary was meager.

And since Chris hadn't worked in years and my nieces and nephew, who were his brother's kids, often needed clothes and school supplies and cash for extracurriculars, I'd never managed to set aside money for an emergency, let alone one like this.

"You excited about having Hattie come home? It's been at least two years since I've seen her."

Now I didn't have to remind myself to smile. "Thrilled. It's been too long." My sister, who was five years younger than me, was headed back to town for three weeks for the first time in a year. She'd dreamed of working for Doctors Without Borders since the moment she'd heard about it as a child; now that's exactly what she was doing. Since I didn't have the same kind of big dreams, there was no question that she would be the one to finish college and go on to medical school while I took over the family business. Did I love it? No. But I couldn't claim that the cannery had ruined my life. Anyway, at least I had a life to ruin. That was more than my parents could say. "She's going to be so happy to see you tomorrow." Jessalyn was one of our regulars at the Christmas party.

"Me, too. How lucky we are that she's coming home. After all, the real gift of the holidays is being with the ones you love."

"That's true." At least it sounded true. I was having a hard time not imagining Jessalyn's face when she learned she wouldn't be able to pay her rent. Or envisioning Reggie, who'd been at the cannery nearly as long and who had three foster kids in addition to his two adult children, being told at the grocery store that his debit card didn't work. I pictured Hattie—my sensible, plan-ahead sister—aghast when I confessed that I hadn't saved enough to deal with a problem like this.

Thankfully, Jessalyn hadn't picked up on the angst that had come over me again. "Isn't it? Merry Christmas to you, Bailey George."

I swallowed the lump in my throat. "Merry Christmas to you, too, Jessalyn."

***

Billie had taken off right after delivering the bad news, and all of the employees had left the factory, too. But I sat in my office for—well, I don't know how long exactly, but it was a good long time. I combed through the spreadsheets and payroll documents. I checked and double-checked the cannery's bank balance and called the company that managed my retirement account to see if I could drain it to pay everyone (no dice, and anyway, I hadn't socked away nearly enough to make a difference). Finally, I gave myself a few minutes to cry over the impossibility of our financial future before locking up, fully aware that this might be the last time I shut the cannery's doors behind me.

After I got into my car, I reached for my phone. I needed to talk to someone other than my aunt about the pickle we were in. My mom always knew the right thing to say or do, which was why she'd been beloved by everyone who knew her. I guess after she died I figured one day I'd grow up to be like her. All these years later I was still waiting for that to happen, and talking to her wasn't an option.

I was about to call Chris when I realized that I already knew how he was going to react. Things between us had been strained for the past couple of months. Heck, the past couple of years. Just the night before, we'd gotten into an argument because he'd asked me what I wanted for Christmas. I'd been incredulous: "You're just now shopping for me?" Which, of course, had made him pace around the house muttering. "You want me to *not* get you anything? I don't understand you sometimes, Bailey. Actually, I do. I can't give you a baby, so nothing else will ever be good enough."

I climbed into bed after he said that, even though it was barely eight o'clock. Then I pulled the duvet cover over my head so Chris wouldn't see me cry. I wasn't crying because he was wrong, but because he was right. The only thing I wanted *was* a child—at one point I'd had my heart set on three. The doctors couldn't figure out why we couldn't conceive, but after years and years of trying, it was evident that it was never going to happen for us.

I wished I knew what had caused the chasm in our marriage. There was the issue of our infertility, sure. But Chris's waning enthusiasm for—well, if not our relationship, then our life, cut deeper than that. Now if we talked, it was to disagree, and if we let that continue for more than two minutes, we ended up in a fight that would leave us both stewing for days. When I suggested we go to couples' therapy, he'd looked at me like I'd just proposed waxing all of his body hair as slowly as possible.

Anyway, Chris thought Billie was, quote, "a train wreck." By keeping her on at the cannery, I'd been asking for a disaster, or so he'd claim. Maybe so, but blaming her wasn't going to fix this.

I didn't know what *would* fix it. Probably nothing. And the sooner I accepted that, the sooner I could move on. But moving on would mean shuttering the whole operation, a possibility that had been looming like an ominous shadow for a while. Now I realized that I'd just delayed the inevitable—and at the worst possible time of year. Credit card bills for all those Christmas presents would be due soon. Heating bills, too, and with the cold front that had yet to let up, they'd be brutal. Then there was the fact that jobs were so scarce in this part of the state that my employees might have to move elsewhere to find employment. Which meant our community would shrink even more than it already had over the past decade.

I could see my breath in the car, so I cranked up the

heat, which was still blowing cold, then called Lacy, my best friend. Lacy and I were as different as two people could be. I'd been married for more than a decade; she hadn't had a long-term relationship that entire time. I wore jeans and T-shirts most days; Lacy, who worked remotely as a marketing specialist for a company based in Manhattan, was always dressed to the nines. But we'd been inseparable since junior high school, when I'd found her hiding in the bathroom after a boy pinched her backside on the way to class. I'd linked arms with her, marched her back into the hall, and pushed the boy directly into his locker—sealing our friendship. Lacy's personal life was often in shambles, so she wasn't the kind of person you'd call for advice. But she was funny and irreverent, and she of all people would know how to perk me up.

She picked up on the second ring. "Bailey, hi. What's up?" She was huffing and puffing, which told me she was exercising. She'd been obsessed with maintaining her size-zero frame as long as I'd known her. During college, she got so thin that I could count her ribs, and I'd told her I was worried about how far she was taking her dieting.

She didn't talk to me for two months after that, but then my parents died and the next time I saw her, she looked markedly healthier and informed me that we were never going to fight about something as stupid as body fat ever again. And we hadn't. Still, Lacy's weight fixation usually got worse when she was dating someone, which she hadn't been in a few months. With cookies and cocktails at every turn—not to mention run-ins with relatives and exes, of which Lacy had many—maybe the holidays had triggered her.

"Are you really on the elliptical right now, when I'm planning to eat an entire gingerbread house and wash it down with eggnog? By which I mean a pint of bourbon?"

"Oh." She exhaled, then inhaled sharply. "Yeah. You headed home?"

My windshield was still half-frosted with crystalline ice, and the vents had yet to blow warm air. It was an exceptionally bitter December, even for the Northeast. I'd be lucky if I left the parking lot in the next ten minutes. "Not anytime soon, I'm afraid."

"Great. Listen . . ."

Something about the way she said "listen" told me she would not be cheering me up this afternoon, and fresh sadness washed over me. "I'm kind of in a bad way, Lace. I was hoping you could talk."

"Awww, Bae. You know I'm here for you. But I need to wrap this up real quick. Maybe we can hit Clarence's later?" Clarence's was our local watering hole. It was a dive, but it was *our* dive, and it had been a town fixture since my mom's grandparents had moved to this sleepy part of New York after World War II.

"Sure." I felt deflated, and it occurred to me that she'd been almost as distant as Chris lately. Her detachment was a relatively new phenomenon. She was usually all over me like white on rice during the holidays, because she knew how hard they were for me. "Why don't you call me when you're on your way?"

"You're the best!" It sounded like her aerobic capacity had just spontaneously doubled.

I was about to say, "No, you are," because that was our shtick, when she hung up.

"Okay then." The windshield had finally defrosted

and I decided to take that as a sign to get the heck out of there. I rubbed my gloved hands together one more time, then hit the gas.

A few minutes later, I pulled up in front of my house. But I headed to the house next door, where my husband's brother, Tony, lived with his three kids, Chet, DeeDee, and Jane. I almost always stopped at their place before I went home. Because Tony . . . well, he was the worst. He'd been a big football star back in the day. Now he was bald and bloated, which I wouldn't mention if he weren't so bitter about it. Tony worked at the cannery, too. And though he was one of our lowest performers, I continued to keep him on because family was family and I didn't want to find out what he'd do for money if I fired him. He was the kind of guy who saw a pretty woman and made it his mission to take her down a notch, which was probably one reason his wife, Deanna, had disappeared in the middle of the night four years earlier. I still don't know what possessed her to leave the kids behind, though. They were great little people who I hoped would grow up to be even better adults one day, yet Tony treated them like they were the reason he limped through life like someone covered with festering wounds. That's why I made it a habit of showing up unannounced at their place as often as possible—to remind him that I was watching, and to let Chet, DeeDee, and Jane know that I loved them.

I headed up the walkway to their beat-up ranch, which was still wearing the same wreath I'd hung on the door last Christmas. Just as I was about to knock, I saw the kids through the small window in the door. Jane was wearing a red and white Santa hat, and Chet was chasing DeeDee around, trying to put another one on her head as she squealed with delight. Tony was nowhere to be seen, which may have been why they looked so . . . happy. Almost like Hattie and I had been as kids, before we knew life was going to clobber us by stealing the two people we loved most.

I turned away quickly before my nieces and nephew could see me. I couldn't do it. I just could not face them knowing I was the reason they were about to go broke. I wiped my eyes and tromped across their snow-covered lawn to my own house.

The lights were off in our small Craftsman bungalow, so Chris was probably out doing whatever it was Chris did all day. He'd quit his job as a mechanic seven years ago after his dad died and left him and Tony each a lump of cash. Some of Chris's had gone toward the down payment on our house, but the rest was in a trust that only he had access to. I didn't care all that much about the money. At least unlike Tony, Chris hadn't blown through it at casinos in less than a year. I just wished my husband would find a constructive way to spend his time, like—I don't know, fly fishing, maybe, or cake baking or even joining a fantasy football league. Now he slept in, went to the gym, and for reasons I had yet to identify, constantly left our home looking like a tornado had just touched down in it. I'd only ever admitted this to Lacy, but he'd become a shadow of the charismatic, good-natured guy I'd fallen in love with in high school. I couldn't help but wonder if my being unable to get pregnant had led to his perpetual funk. A few months earlier, I'd sidled up to him in bed and slipped my arm around his waist, cautiously optimistic; it had been ages since we'd made love. But instead of leaning in to kiss me, or even wrap his arms around me, he turned toward the wall. "I hope you're not still thinking the whole kid thing might happen for us. That ship has sailed, Bailey."

I hadn't been thinking about "the whole kid thing," but it still felt like the cruelest thing anyone had ever said to me, and I didn't speak to him for two days afterward. Worse, he hadn't seemed to notice.

I let myself in the house quietly, kicked off my snowy boots on the mat beside the door and hung up my parka. There was a pounding noise coming from upstairs, and in spite of everything, my spirits rose. I'd been begging Chris to put together the dresser I'd bought at Ikea six months earlier. A functioning piece of plywood furniture wasn't my idea of a stellar Christmas present, but if Chris was feeling energized enough to pull out a hammer, maybe he would be in the right frame of mind to help me figure out what to do about Billie draining the company's bank account.

Whoa, Chris must be working awfully hard, I thought as I climbed the stairs to our room. The thumping was growing louder, and he moaned like he'd hurt himself. I immediately felt bad for the thoughts I'd been having about our marriage. Hattie would have been proud of me. She and I talked once or twice a month when her connection was good enough, and she was always telling me to focus on the positive, not the negative. Maybe she was right. So Chris was grumpy and uninterested. At least he was finally trying to turn things around.

I was at the end of the hall when I heard another voice that wasn't Chris's. Had he invited someone over to help him build the dresser? Ikea furniture could be complicated, I conceded, recalling the time Chris had hammered his thumb trying to put together a TV stand.

The minute I opened the bedroom door, my eyes stopped communicating with my brain. On the one hand, I could see that there were a couple of buck-naked people on my bed. And yet it took another twenty to thirty seconds to process that the back facing me belonged to Lacy, and that the hairy white legs sticking out from beneath her were Chris's.

The sound that came out of my mouth then was nothing like any sound I'd made before. But Lacy kept moving up and down like a miniature carousel horse on top of Chris, completely oblivious to my presence. The bed was directly across from the door, so Chris couldn't see me behind Lacy. He must have heard me, though, because he bent his knees and tried to peer around her.

I glanced around, wide-eyed and feral. I needed to do something. Fast. But nothing in our bedroom—not the vase on the dresser with the dried roses from a bouquet Chris had given me years earlier; not our wedding portrait on the wall; not even the hideous plaid blanket draped over the armchair, which Chris refused to replace, even though it held no sentimental value—would do the trick. I ran to the bathroom, reached under the sink, and grabbed the fire extinguisher.

It had been there since we moved in, so I had no idea if it worked.

I positioned myself in the doorway, pulled the pin out of the extinguisher, squeezed the handle, and blanketed my husband and best friend in carcinogenic white foam as they screamed and scrambled out of bed.

They were jumping up and down like I'd lit them on fire, not rendered them inflammable. But maybe because they weren't wearing clothes and I was still holding a large metal object that could have doubled as a weapon in a pinch, neither made a move to stop me. It was like deep down, they understood that they deserved it.

In less than a minute, the whole place looked like a winter wonderland. I'd probably ruined our bedroom, if not the top half of the house. So be it. Even in my frozen, barely functioning state, I'd already decided I was never coming back there again.

I threw the extinguisher on the bed and looked at them one more time, these people I had loved and trusted.

Then I fled.

THREE

When the ground beneath you shifts, you search for something constant to keep you steady. Chris and Lacy had been that for me after my parents died. Chris and I had only been dating off and on for two years; he'd remained in town to attend community college and we'd seen each other every other weekend. But he'd been the one to drive me to Cornell that January to pick up my things from my dorm. When we arrived at my parents' house that night, he stayed over, and without any discussion, he moved in the next day. We were never really apart again.

Lacy was at NYU at the time, but she called me every morning and every night, no matter what was going on, for three straight years. She never said as much, but I think she wanted to make sure I wouldn't hurt myself. At the very least, she tried to keep me from falling too far down the rabbit hole before she could catch me. Granted, there was no real chance that I'd give in to my grief; someone had to care for Hattie, who was in her sophomore year of high school. Yet Lacy's phone calls—even if they only lasted a few minutes—were a lifeline for me. Looking back, the two of them were the only reason I made it through that dark period without losing my mind.

But now the two people who had always been my constant had moved the ground beneath my feet. The more I thought about it, the less I understood what I'd just seen. It was . . . gross, for starters. But it was also the most horrible betrayal I could think. How could they? Why would they? Had either of them ever loved me at all? For the first time in my short and unspectacular life, I envied my parents, who no longer had to deal with all the ways that human existence can chew you up and spit you out.

Lacy called me minutes after I got back in my car. Maybe because I was still on autopilot, I picked up before I could realize what I was doing.

"Bailey! I am so sorry! It didn't mean anything!"

"The lies?" My voice was as dry as the Sahara. "The duplicity? Because it means a whole lot to me."

She sounded like she was on the verge of

hyperventilating. "I know you won't understand this, but it was just sex. For both of us. Chris doesn't love me."

"Well, that's super reassuring."

"Bailey, please. I really am so sorry."

I pressed my eyes shut. "Never speak to me again, Lacy. Good luck with your life."

The minute I ended the call, Chris's name appeared on the screen. I wondered if they were still side-by-side in the bedroom. Or maybe wrapped in towels in the bathroom, discussing how they were going to sweep the shards of my life under the rug. I declined Chris's call, as well as the next three.

I was too numb to cry as I sped away from the house. In fact, I had absolutely no idea what to do with myself. I almost headed back to the cannery, but I couldn't bear it— not when I knew it would be closed for good by the time this year became the next, and that all of those people I cared for would be in the red.

Really, the more I thought about it, the more I loathed myself. Billie may have been the one to empty the bank account, but I'd given her access to it. Everything my parents had built would crumble because I'd swapped common sense for an idiot's blind trust—just like my aunt had when she agreed to her former flame's harebrained plan. No wonder Chris had lost interest in me, then cheated on me with the artist formerly known as my best friend. He probably understood that I was too dumb to realize what was happening right under my own nose. Well, he hadn't been wrong about that. Lacy's car had been parked right at the end of my block and I hadn't even noticed it until I was speeding away from the scene of their crime!

This may sound strange, but I actually wished I hadn't come home early. If only I could have made it through the holidays without knowing that my already-small family had just grown even smaller, then maybe I wouldn't feel like . . .

Well, like not going on.

I drove right past Clarence's, but once I was a few blocks away, I decided I didn't have anywhere better to be. I did a U-turn and pulled into the bar's parking lot, feeling like the weariness of the whole world was on my shoulders. Better to go have a drink now, I decided; it wouldn't be long before everyone knew about the cannery's demise and I wouldn't be welcome there anymore.

"Bailey George, you're a sight for sore eyes." Clarence himself was behind the long mahogany bar, pouring whiskey into a tumbler. Apparently, I wasn't the only one stocking up on liquid courage in preparation for the next couple of days, because it wasn't even five yet and the place was already bustling.

He slid the glass toward me. "Thanks, Clarence. You've got the sore part right. How'd you know I needed this?"

Clarence's eyes crinkled at the corners as he smiled at me. "Call it a hunch. You work at a place like this long enough and you get to knowing who needs what and when." His father had started the bar, but Clarence, who'd inherited both his name and his business, had been in charge since I was a kid. "Also, your aunt stopped by earlier, though she didn't stay long."

"Oh." I looked down at my drink for a second. "What'd she tell you?"

"That she'd just landed you both in some deep doo-doo." He nodded sagely. "And since I'm a vault, that's all

I'll say about that."

"Never change, Clarence." I tossed back the deep amber liquid in one throat-burning gulp. Whooo. It was as strong as lighter fluid, but I felt at least four percent better than I had before. I plopped my glass back on the bar. "Another, please."

Clarence raised an eyebrow, but reached for the bottle.

"Don't worry, I'll get a taxi."

He held out a weathered hand. "Keys, Ms. George."

I pulled them out of my bag and put them in his palm. "I'll come back for the car—"

I almost said tomorrow, but the very idea of facing the following day was sorrow-inducing. What was the point of Christmas Eve now? What was the point of anything? Clarence had filled my glass again, so instead of finishing my sentence, I finished my drink.

Roger Murphy was at the other side of the bar, waving at Clarence like he'd croak if he didn't get a beer in the next ten seconds. Clarence glanced at me quickly. "I'll be back. Don't get into any trouble, you hear?"

I was glad he left before I could tell him that it was too

late for that.

I set some cash on the bar for my drinks, intending to go walk off my buzz, even if it meant risking a toe or three to frostbite. But one perk—or drawback, depending on how you look at it—of being the person who employs half the town is that there's never a shortage of free booze being sent your way.

Or maybe everyone just felt bad because they knew tomorrow was the anniversary of my parents' death.

At any rate, Arjun Patel bought me my third whiskey before I even put my coat on. Then Betty Lewis sent over another. "To the boss!" She raised her glass and everyone all the way down the bar lifted their glasses to cheer me.

As I raised my glass to them, all the tears I'd been holding back sprung to the surface. If only they knew what a disappointment their boss really was. They would soon enough.

The room had just started to spin ever so slightly when Clarence leaned across the bar to peer at me. "You okay, Ms. George? You're looking a bit peaked."

"I'm fine, Clarence." I may or may not have been

slurring, but I *was* fine, even if I had forgotten the point of my brief and lackluster life. I'd ruined my parents' business, which they'd put their blood, sweat, and tears into for more than three decades. Every detail, from the machinery to the canning labels to the health-care plans they offered the employees, had been chosen with care. Now their dreams were about to disappear like kindling in a raging fire.

And my husband—my partner of twenty-one years, more than half my time on earth!—had given up on the family I'd always wanted. Then my so-called best friend had decided to play naked Twister with him.

I stared into my empty glass, wishing it could give me the answers I desperately needed. For example, when, exactly, had Chris decided I was unlovable? I'd tried so hard to be a good wife, just like my mom had been to my dad; he, in turn, had made her his whole world. At first, that's what Chris and I seemed to have, too. He helped me raise Hattie. He supported me at the factory and shared my dreams of having a family and carrying on what my parents had started.

Somewhere along the way, those dreams began to fray

at the edges. And Chris became someone else.

Still, I never nagged him about all the housework he refused to do. I didn't say a word about the fact that although he paid for half the mortgage, he refused to cover his share of the utilities—even though he was the one who sat home all day, running up the electricity bill. At our wedding, he'd vowed to be the best version of himself for his beloved wife.

Maybe the person he was now *was* the best version of him.

Or maybe I'd given him permission to be a big old man-child. This, like everything else, was on me.

What did Lacy see in Chris, anyway? I knew what he saw in her. She had a pert little nose, full rosy lips, and a way of making every man feel like he was the center of the universe. But what was he to her?

Probably a conquest, I concluded. It didn't even make me feel better to know she'd tire of him just as he started to fall in love with her. It was always the same: she couldn't stand being too close to someone; she couldn't bear being truly happy. Whenever things were getting good, she would go and blow them up.

Apparently, that tendency to self-destruct now extended to her friendships.

"Bailey? Bailey George, is that you?" Someone was calling me. It wasn't Clarence, or any other voice I recognized. I spun around on my barstool with the grace of a drunken water buffalo and got my boot stuck beneath the footrest.

Oh no, I thought, as I started tipping over. *Timber*—

"Hey. There you go."

Someone caught me. Someone with very strong arms who happened to be the spitting image of Ryan Reynolds. *Was* that Ryan Reynolds? How drunk was I, exactly? I managed to mumble "thanks" to the mysterious handsome stranger who apparently knew my name.

"It's the least I can do. You okay?"

I stood and heaved myself back onto my bar seat. "Define 'okay.'"

He laughed. "I see you haven't lost your sense of humor."

I frowned as I took in his sandy brown hair and warm

brown eyes. He was wearing a plaid button-down shirt and dark jeans. Compared with Chris, whose uniform consisted of ratty T-shirts and sweatpants, he was dressed like a male model. And I guess he did look familiar—and yet I couldn't pull his name out of the corners of my mind. Did I know him?

"You do."

Heaven help me, was I so drunk my thoughts were leaking right out of my mouth?

"Yeah, they are. And you're still doing it." He was smiling at me, and for some reason, my brain's response was to smile right back at him. "You don't recognize me, huh? Nate Hatch. We went to high school together."

"Nate . . ." I waited for my neurons to connect. It took an alarmingly long time, but then, finally, it hit me. "Nate Hatch? The tuba player that . . ."

"Everyone called Tubby?" He was still smiling, but I still felt like I'd just wedged both of my feet into my mouth.

"Argh, I'm sorry. Kids are awful. But. Um." He looked different. Really different. I hated to be vain, but he'd traded at least eighty pounds of extra weight for forty of lean muscle. And his face . . . well, I just didn't remember him looking like that.

"Yeah, I had a nose job." He laughed. "And I got acquainted with the gym. But I still play the tuba."

"Oh, I bet you do." I grimaced. "Sorry. I'm a bit tipsy. I've had a really bad . . ." I almost said "day," but that wasn't quite right. "Life."

"Come on now, that can't be true. I'm still in touch with Buddy and Josh—you remember them?"

Of course I did—they both worked for me. I nodded.

"They said you're great."

I glanced down the bar, where I could spot at least ten different people who were also in my employ—or at least they were until they found out the terrible thing I'd allowed to happen. "They won't be saying that for long."

He frowned. Somehow, he looked even better-looking with a furrowed brow. "How so?"

"It's kind of a long story."

"I've got time." The guy seated next to me had just left, so Nate hopped onto his barstool.

I may have been on my way to being plastered, but I

still wasn't going to tell this near-stranger my terrible tale. "How about we start with you? What in the heck are you doing in town?"

His grin felt like the sun on my skin. "I just moved back."

"From?"

"L.A."

Just outside the window, snow was blowing sideways. Maybe that's why I didn't try to speed our conversation along. "Now why would you do something like that?"

"The weather wasn't half bad. The surgeons, either." He put a finger to the bridge of his nose and winked. Man, he was good-looking. "But that whole 'location, location, location' thing doesn't matter if your location doesn't have the right people in it. My folks are still here and they're not getting any younger. And my sister has a gaggle of kids that barely know who I am. I'm trying to change that."

"LuAnne, right?" I remembered his sister—she was in Hattie's class. I saw her pushing a double stroller around the park sometimes.

"You got it. What about you?" He was very close to

me, so it was hard not to notice that he smelled nice. Sort of like laundry detergent, but laundry detergent for men. "You still married to Chris Cross?"

"Pardon?" Chris's last name was Crawford.

"Sorry—I'm being a jerk. We used to call him Chris Cross in high school."

"We?"

"The nerds. He wasn't exactly nice back then."

I almost laughed, but I couldn't manage it. Not when the image of my husband—philandering and coated in fire retardant—was so fresh in my mind. "Yeah, that hasn't changed much."

Clarence had appeared in front of us. "Mr. Hatch. Would you like your usual?"

"Yes, sir."

I eyed them. "You two know each other?"

Clarence winked at Nate, who saluted him. "We go back a ways."

"Weird, but okay." I looked down into my empty glass. "Just one more for me, Clarence."

He cocked his head and looked at me with kindness.

"You sure, Ms. George?"

"More sure about that than I am anything else." Which wasn't saying a lot.

"How about we make it a whiskey soda, heavy on the soda? You'll thank me tomorrow."

I sighed. "Okay. Thank you today, and tomorrow."

Nate took the drink that Clarence had just handed to him and lifted it. "To new old friends."

"Cheers." But no sooner had I clinked my glass against his than one tear escaped, then another, and I had to cover my eyes with my hands for a second. "Sorry. My contacts are bothering me." I hoped he wouldn't examine me too closely and discover that I didn't wear contacts.

When I looked up again, Nate was peering at me curiously. "Have to say, I'm surprised to hear you and Chris ended up together." It was after dinnertime now and the bar had gone from bustling to too crowded; he had to speak loudly so I could hear him.

"Yeah, well, like our time on this spinning orb we call our planet, it'll be over soon."

"It?"

"Our marriage. Turns out I have very bad taste in humans."

Nate shook his head. "I'm sorry to hear that about your marriage. But you're way too hard on yourself."

"No, I'm not hard enough. That's the problem."

"That's nuts—but tell me more." He was a good listener, that Nate Hatch, and I wasn't just saying that because of his fine face and his gravity-defying rear end, which I'd stolen a glance at when he was saving me from splatting on the bar's Formica floor.

"You want the quick and dirty version, or the long and ugly one?"

"Whichever version you want to tell."

"As I discovered this afternoon, Chris has been spelunking in my best friend's cave."

His eyes got big. "Lacy?"

"The one and only. You know, you have an awfully good memory, given that we graduated twenty years ago."

"My memory's pretty rotten, actually. I just keep up on social media."

"Ah." Then I closed my eyes, which was a bad idea.

Clarence had put music on. "Jingle Bell Rock" had just ended and Judy Garland was warbling about faithful friends and how someday soon we'd all be together, and—well, it was just too much.

"Hey. Hey, Bailey." Nate was touching my arm. "You want to get out of here?"

I wasn't sure what was more mortifying: that I'd started drunkenly crying in the middle of the bar in front of a hot acquaintance and half my employees; or that I appeared so vulnerable that said acquaintance thought now was the perfect opportunity to have his way with me.

"You don't even know me." I sniffled. "And I'm married. At least for now."

"I'm aware of both things, and I wasn't suggesting we—you know." Even in the low light of the bar, I could tell he was blushing. It was way cuter than I wanted to admit. "I was just thinking we could go get a cup of coffee and help you sober up."

"Oh." Well, that was kind of disappointing, even if I appreciated that he was a decent person. They seemed to be in short supply lately. "Coffee sounds good, but what I really need . . ." I hiccupped. "Is to find a hotel to crash at tonight."

"Wait, what? Don't you live here?"

I glanced around. "In the bar?"

"In town, silly."

"Oh. Yeah. But I can't go home ever again." I guess I could have gone to Tony's, but Chris's brother was one of the last people I wanted to look at right about now. I suddenly felt incredibly sad, not just for myself, but for my Chet, DeeDee, and Jane. They were about to face serious financial struggles that were all my fault. Just as bad, I'd probably rarely see them now that I'd have to ask Chris for a . . .

Divorce.

Just thinking the word felt like a knife straight to my heart.

I looked at Nate. Unless I squinted, there were two of him now, and while that wasn't unpleasant, that was definitely my cue. "You know, I think it's time for me to take a little walk."

He frowned. "Where to?"

"Somewhere. Anywhere. Maybe the river." I pulled my parka on and started for the door. Outside, snow was coming down in thick, wet flakes; the whole downtown area looked almost exactly like the way I'd left my bedroom a few hours earlier. Where would I go? Where would I sleep? It didn't really matter. In a couple of hours, it would officially be Christmas Eve. By ruining the 23rd, too, Chris had turned my annual trauma into a two-day holiday.

"Bailey. Let me at least walk you to a hotel."

"Sorry, but noooo." Now Judy Garland wasn't the only one warbling. "It's been nice re-meeting you, Nate, but now I must go . . . somewhere other than here."

And with that, I flung open the door and wandered out into the cold, dark night.

FOUR

I still don't remember how I got there, but somehow I ended up at my parents' house. A young couple had bought it from me and Hattie years ago because she needed money for medical school and Chris and I had decided to move in together.

Now the couple had kids, and I stood on the sidewalk, cold to the bone and crusted with snow, and watched them through the brightly lit windows of my old home. A little girl was running as her dad chased her with a giant stuffed bear. After a few laps around the dining room table, he caught her and tossed her up in the air as she laughed and laughed. Then the mom came in with a baby hoisted on her hip, and she and the dad kissed under the mistletoe hanging in the archway between the dining and living rooms.

And I started to cry again.

I would never have a family like that. Even if Chris

hadn't cheated on me, we still weren't going to have children, which had pretty much been my only dream. It wasn't right that people like Tony—who treated the three fantastic humans he'd made like they were nothing but nuisances—could procreate, and I couldn't.

But mostly I really missed my parents. My dad had been a big, jolly guy, the kind the neighbors called when a pipe burst or when they couldn't figure out how to talk sense into one of their teenagers. He knew all kinds of stuff, but he never made you feel like you were wrong for not knowing it, too. He was good like that. And my mom . . .

Well, she was the best person I'd ever known. She was unflaggingly kind, even to people who didn't deserve it. If Hattie or I broke something, she didn't ask what we'd done. Instead, she immediately called to see if we were okay. There was no such thing as an unfixable problem in Celia George's mind. If only she were here now, to help me figure out how to fix the mess I'd landed us all in.

"It isn't fair," I said to the sky. It was still dumping snow all over the place, but I could see a sprinkling of stars between the ominous winter clouds, and I decided that they were listening to me. "It's like the better you try to be, the more you suffer. Why else would my mom and dad die while they were still in their prime? Why would my reward for being a wonderful wife be an unfaithful husband? Who, for the record, has spent the past several years doing his best impersonation of a sloth? And what about all of the cannery employees? They show up every day and do work that a lot of people might stick their noses up at. But they take pride in putting food on other people's plates. Now they're going to struggle to do the same for their own families."

I stared up at the darkness for a good long while, not bothering to wipe the tears from my eyes, even though I could feel my eyelashes turning into tiny icicles. Work. Family. Life itself. I just couldn't see the point to any of it.

"Bailey."

I have no idea how long I'd been attempting to freeze myself to death when I heard Nate call my name. Long enough that all that whiskey I'd had at Clarence's had made its way through my bloodstream, plus, I hadn't had a meal since, oh, lunch. Which is to say I was good and drunk, and

I stumbled a little as I turned to face him.

"What'r you doin' here?"

He shoved his hands in the pockets of his coat. "Checking on you."

Why were men in scarves so cute? Why didn't their red noses look ridiculous? Okay, I was forced to admit that it was just Nate's surgically sculpted nose that didn't look ridiculous, as I could recall plenty of times when Chris resembled Rudolph with a raging sinus infection.

"Aren't you going to go in?" Nate was staring at me expectantly.

"Go in where?" I was confused.

"Your parents' place? I checked the hotel, but when they said you weren't registered there, I figured you'd end up crashing here."

"There is no here."

"Huh?"

I gestured toward the house. "My parents don't live here anymore. Because . . ." Even beneath the dim streetlight, I could see that he was looking at me too intently, and I had to turn away. "Um. They're dead."

"Oh." He was in front of me now, and he reached out for my arm. Though there were layers of nylon, down alternative, and wool between us, it still felt surprisingly good to be touched by another person. I was more starved for attention than I'd realized. "I'm so sorry for your loss. That's awful. Josh and Buddy never mentioned it. Is that why you ended up running the cannery?"

If by "running it" he meant "running it into the ground," then sure. "Yeah."

"Well, can you stay with Hattie tonight?"

I shook my head. "She's probably in the middle of her layover in Spain right now. She flies into JFK tomorrow morning and then takes the train up."

Now confusion was written all over his face. "From where?"

"Oh—sorry. Afghanistan. She's a doctor. She works over there." Even saying this aloud made me feel ashamed. My younger sister was spending her days saving the world—well, at least some of the world. And here I was, destroying the tiny little corner of the planet that I had any impact on. I knew I was in the middle of throwing myself a one-woman pity party, but I couldn't help it. It was like I was just seeing clearly for the first time, and the picture before my eyes was like a funhouse mirror filled with never-ending horrors.

"I didn't realize that." He narrowed his eyes and looked at me. "So, if you're not going home and you can't stay here, where exactly are you headed?"

I could have gone to Billie's, but she hadn't picked up when I drunk dialed her in the bar. I'd since realized that I wasn't ready to see her and explain that I'd figured absolutely nothing out since we'd last spoke. "I was going to walk over to the bridge." Never mind that I was pretty sure my pinky toes would have to be amputated if I stayed outside even another three minutes.

"And do what, exactly?"

Throw myself over the edge and see what happened?

"You're muttering to yourself again."

"Gosh darn it."

"You okay?" He'd put his arm around me.

"Mmmhmm." Woo-hoo. I needed a tall glass of water, a handful of ibuprofen, and at least twenty-four hours in bed.

Or, you know. A complete do-over on my miserable existence.

"Good. How about you stay at my place tonight?" He smiled at me. "No funny business. You need a good night's sleep, and I have a comfortable sofa."

That sounded better than anything else I'd come up with. "Where is your place, exactly?"

"Not far."

I looked at the house I'd grown up in one more time. Then I turned back to Nate.

"Let's go."

***

Nate's apartment complex was an old factory that had been converted. He had a loft on the top floor. It was large, as lofts tend to be, with lots of windows that looked out over the town and the cannery, down the block. I stood in front of them and gazed out at Main Street. The buildings were all decorated with twinkle lights, and I could see the large Christmas tree and menorah on the center of the square.

My frozen extremities had finally started to thaw, but

the floor felt like a waterbed beneath my feet as I turned back to him. "You . . . own this place?"

He was arranging some pillows and a quilt on his sofa. "Just renting. I'm going to look for a house to buy soon."

"Awfully nice for a rental. You make it big in acting or something?"

He laughed. "Or something. The sofa's all made up, but are you sure you don't want my bed?"

"No, but thanks. I don't know why you're being so nice to me, but I appreciate it."

"Don't mention it."

I lowered myself onto the sofa. Only then did I realize I was so tired you'd think I'd just run a marathon or given birth. (Not that I knew what either of those things felt like, but still.) "Okay, I won't mention it."

"Good. You know where the bathroom is." He gestured toward the kitchen. "And please help yourself to anything you want. But since you're already getting settled in, can I get you anything before I hit the hay?"

He's a really nice guy, I thought to myself. Of course, I'd once believed that of Chris, too. Or had I? I couldn't remember anymore. Chris had called me no fewer than a dozen times since I'd left the house. I listened to one of his many messages on the walk to Nate's, expecting to hear a sobbing apology. Instead, he sounded upset that I wasn't returning his calls, so on impulse, I blocked his number. What did we have left to talk about?

Nothing. Not a damn thing.

"No, but thank you."

Nate smiled at me from the end of the sofa. "Then good night, Bailey. I'm just in the other room if you need anything."

Maybe I said good night back to him; maybe I didn't. My eyes closed, which seemed like a good idea until Chris and Lacy immediately appeared on the movie screen in my mind. They were still eating forbidden fruit in their birthday suits, but this time they were looking at me and pointing and laughing.

I pulled the quilt over my head, just in case Nate was still in the room, because I didn't want him to witness my drunken sobbing.

When I stopped crying, I glanced around in the dark,

suddenly alarmed at how readily I'd agreed to sleep over. After all, given how broken my people radar was, it was entirely possible Nate wasn't a nice guy at all, but an ax murderer.

So be it, I decided after a moment. Being put out of my misery would probably be the best Christmas present of all.

Technically I didn't want my life to be over. But I'm ashamed to say that my last thought before my consciousness mercifully turned off was:

It would have been so much easier if I'd never been born.

FIVE

The next thing I knew, it was Christmas Eve—the day I dreaded all year, which I'd probably made even worse by getting over-served the night before.

But as I sat up on Nate's sofa, I didn't feel hungover. That was weird, but maybe it was because I'd stuck to whiskey all night. I pried open my sleep-crusted eyes and glanced around. The place looked . . . different. It was sparsely decorated to begin with, but all of his boxes were gone. He must have stayed up late or gotten up early to unpack, I decided.

I didn't want to call out for him, in case he was still sleeping, so I crept across the living room to the kitchen. He'd told me to help myself, and I was starving. But the fridge was . . . empty. How odd. And the cupboards were, too.

I froze and listened for snoring or rustling or some other evidence that Nate was here.

No dice.

Was this some kind of weird setup? Maybe he didn't even live here. It wouldn't be a surprise, given that these same stellar people-reading skills had led me to trust my aunt, who—however lovable and well-intentioned—had the business acumen of a toddler. And of course, Chris and Lacy had probably been doing the deed for months without me noticing that anything was amiss. I might as well have been strolling around with a bull's-eye on my back.

The weight of the past twenty-four hours came crashing down on me, and I had to grab the edge of the granite counter to brace myself.

Once I was steady again, I poured myself a glass of water, though what I really needed was a full pot of coffee. I couldn't find a piece of paper or a pen to scribble a note to Nate—and come to think of it, I didn't have his phone number, either. Maybe I could get his information from Clarence and text him later on.

For now, I had things to do.

I grabbed my coat and purse from the armchair, slipped into my boots, and quietly let myself out.

The night before, the town had been sparkling and white. Now it all looked as gray as the side of a highway. I wondered if it was some weird effect of global warming.

I sighed heavily and trudged through the slush.

I couldn't go home, so I headed to the diner to get something to eat, then track down my car so I could pick up Hattie from the train station. Unfortunately, getting to the diner meant walking past the cannery, but it was bitterly cold, and going the long way around would add nearly half a mile to my trip. Not an option, I thought, my teeth chattering.

I found myself recalling five years earlier, when I'd secured a major contract with a giant food and beverage company. The cannery had desperately needed a new client, and this was a big one that brought job security—and a pay increase—for our workers. Billie and I had run around the factory handing out sparkling wine in Dixie cups, and everyone cheered and toasted to our good fortune. Little did I know that just a few years later, the company would cut its rate, swearing it was a onetime thing. Six months later they did it again, leaving me struggling to pay my employees even as the company's CEO took home a multimillion-dollar paycheck.

As I came upon the factory, a jolt of fear shot through me. Several of the windows had been broken, and the sign over the door that read "George's Cannery" was missing. Word must have spread about our finances. But would our employees really be so angry that they'd loot their own workplace? It seemed completely unlike anyone—even Tony—to do that.

I looked for the factory keys in my purse, and remembered that they were on the keychain I'd handed to Clarence the night before. The windows of the cannery were too high for me to peer through. Still, I knew something was wrong; the place didn't smell right. For better or worse, you could catch a whiff of peas or corn from or veggie medley from down the block, no matter what the season. Now all I could smell was—well, I couldn't tell what it was, but something industrial, like spilled oil.

"Spare some change?" A woman wearing several coats and a thick wool hat was huddled in the doorway beneath dirty blankets. "Or are you another one of those scrooges?"

She looked up at me as she said this. It took me a moment to realize I recognized her. She looked twice her age.

"Jessalyn?!"

She frowned from beneath the brim of her hat. "Do I know you?"

I stared at her with disbelief. "It's me, Bailey . . . your boss?"

She snorted. "Boss! I haven't had one of those since two thousand and one."

"Pardon?"

"You must not be from around here." She gestured around. "The George family sold this place to some other company. They went bankrupt after half a year."

The ground beneath me seemed to sway. "What? That can't be."

She shook her head. "If you don't have money for me, I don't have stories for you."

"Um." I fished around my purse until I found a couple of rumpled dollar bills, which I held out to her.

Jessalyn snatched them from my hands. "Thanks,

lady. Storytime's over, but come back later and I'll tell you more."

She really and truly didn't know who I was. Worse, I couldn't shake the feeling that this wasn't some sudden psychic break since I'd last seen her. No: she looked like someone who'd been camped out in that doorway for a very long time.

All of the questions I'd intended to ask her were gone. Finally, I managed to say the only thing I could think of: "Merry Christmas."

"Yeah right." She yanked one of the blankets over her head.

My knees weakened, and I ordered myself to pull it together as I walked away. There had to be an explanation for this.

My parents' old house was on the way to the diner. I'd made that trek hundreds of times over the years before I took over their jobs; I'd sit on the floor in the office I now worked in, doing my homework or sometimes helping my mom with accounting. When I reached their place, I wondered if I'd catch a glimpse of the happy family I'd seen the night before. But the curtains were drawn, and the wreath that had been on the door was gone, too. I shook my head, waiting for the uncanny feeling that had come over me to pass, and continued on my route.

Except as I made my way through town, the feeling only grew stronger. The coffee shop on Main Street, where I'd stopped most days to get my caffeine fix, was boarded up. There was no evidence that my favorite stationery store had ever existed. The post office was still there, but it was a shambles. In the distance, the diner didn't look much better. The worst part was, all of the twinkle lights and holiday decorations I'd seen less than twelve hours earlier were missing. Now, instead of looking like Christmas Eve, it could have been any cold day in March.

I reached into my pocket for my phone, hoping to call someone to find out what had happened. But my pocket was empty, and the phone wasn't in my purse, either. Bad enough that I was clearly losing my mind; now I'd lost my connection to the rest of the world, too?

Deciding a detour was in order, I cut through an alley to get to Clarence's on the next street over. I nearly fainted with relief when I saw the old, familiar neon sign and the bell on the door. It looked like it was open, but the place was empty. Even stranger, my aunt was behind the bar.

"Aunt Billie? What are you doing back there?"

"Can I help you?" She didn't sound unkind, but she lacked her usual warmth.

"You don't recognize me."

"I don't know you." She narrowed her eyes. "I never forget a face."

My heart was galloping in my chest. First Jessalyn, now Billie. What was happening? "It's me, Bailey. Your niece." Suddenly I remembered her teaching me to play the piano. She was so patient, sitting beside me and gently adjusting my fingers when I couldn't find a chord. She'd been much happier as a teacher. If only I had assured her that I could handle running the cannery on my own instead of agreeing to let her come on board.

Well, everyone knows what they say about hindsight.

"I don't know a Bailey, and the only niece I have is Harriet."

I was about to ask her how long that had been true

when a man's gravelly voice rang through the air.

"Babe?" Judd had just come ambling out of the kitchen. Between his red-rimmed eyes and his grease-covered apron and slicked back hair, he looked like he'd just gone for a swim in a deep fryer after pulling an all-nighter. "What's happening out here?"

I eyed him. "Judd? What are you doing here? Where's Clarence?"

Judd didn't answer, but Billie cocked her head and gave me a long, curious look. "He's in the cemetery."

"Doing what?"

Now she stared at me like I was dense. Which maybe wasn't so far off. "Resting."

Clarence was . . . dead? The picture was finally coming into focus, but I didn't like what I was seeing.

"Listen, uh, Bailey. I'm not sure how you know me, but can I get you a drink or what?"

"No, but thanks. Can I ask something really quick, though?"

"I guess."

"What happened to the George family cannery?"

She grunted. "Haven't thought about the cannery in years—and that's no accident."

"Why's that?"

"Not long after my sister and her husband died, that niece I was telling you about? She sold it to some conglomerate who ran the place right into the ground. No other company has even considered setting up shop in this town since, so is it any surprise half of everyone's on unemployment? Don't get me wrong, misery can be good for the bar business—but only if people can actually pay their tabs." She poured some cheap vodka into a shot glass and tossed it back, then wiped her mouth with the back of her arm. "Breakfast is served."

"Um. I. Well, thank you."

"Not sure what you're thanking me for."

I wasn't, either. "All the same, Merry Christmas."

She shook her head sadly. "If you say so."

Stumbling back onto the street like I was the one who'd been doing shots of vodka at ten in the morning, I'd suddenly understood that I'd somehow landed in another reality—one into which I hadn't been born. But instead of making everything better, that had made things much worse.

I realized that my wish had been a grave mistake. Now how was I ever going to get myself—and the rest of our town—back to normal?

SIX

Obviously, the last thing I wanted to do was go see Chris, but I didn't know who else to turn to. Also—this is horrible, but nonetheless the truth—part of me wondered if whatever had turned everything upside down had also erased all of the terrible things that had happened the day before. Maybe my husband had been faithful (however hopeful I was, I understood that it was a stretch to wish he was also happy and productive) and we could start fresh from a reality in which he hadn't stuck his stocking in the Christmas elf I'd called a friend.

My boots were proving to be not nearly as waterproof as they claimed to be, and, as I marched toward my house, snow seeped through their seams. It's tough to stay optimistic when your feet are cold and wet, but I was determined to untangle this strange mess I found myself in, and I picked up my pace a little more.

As I walked, I wondered if Chris and I had ever been

happy—really and truly happy.

Thinking about the plans we had made for a big family, and Chris's dream of starting an auto shop with Tony, I had to admit we had. It was just that somewhere along the way, for reasons I had yet to identify, that happiness had faded.

Ten minutes later, I was in front of my bungalow. It looked more or less the same—in need of a paint job, but not falling apart—which was promising. I knocked on the door, but no one answered. Well, it was technically still my place, wasn't it? I reached for the door handle, and when it turned, I let myself in.

"Hello? Chris? Is anyone here?"

A woman came rushing into the living room where I was standing. I wasn't sure whether to be relieved or devastated that it wasn't Lacy. Then I realized it was . . .

"Hattie?! What are you doing here? I told you I'd pick you up at the train station."

Her eyes bulged. "Ahh! Chriisssss!"

"Hey! Hattie, it's me, Bailey." After what had happened with Jessalyn and Billie, I shouldn't have been surprised that she didn't recognize me . . . except this was my sister. But the sound of her name didn't calm her at all. "Stranger! Stranger danger!"

She was screaming, and beneath her bathrobe, I could she that she was far too thin. And her hair was dyed black, which made her skin look sallow. Mostly, though, her eyes alarmed me.

There was no light in them at all.

"Hattie, you're skin and bones! Are you okay?"

She managed to stop screaming. "Who are you? And why do you keep calling me that?"

"Calling you what?"

"Hattie." She glared at me. "My parents were the only ones who called me that. If someone sent you to remind me of that on the anniversary of their death, that's horrible."

I felt a sob bubble up within me. "I would never do that."

"Harriet? What in God's—" Chris, who'd appeared in the doorway wearing only his boxers and a T-shirt, gave me the once-over. "Who are you?"

"I'm your—" I bit my tongue before I could say

"wife." I looked back and forth between them. "I'm your relative. Are you two together?"

"Ha ha. Tony put you up to this, didn't he? I'm going to murder him."

"This isn't a joke."

"Right, and I'm Kris Kringle." He stuck a thumb out at Hattie. "And this here is Mrs. Klaus."

My stomach dropped. I thought maybe Hattie had been staying with him. It had not once occurred to me that they were married.

Chris glared at me. "Now you'd better get out of our house before we call the cops."

"Hattie." I looked at my sister imploringly. "I know you don't recognize me but look at my face. See any resemblance?" She and I were both the spitting image of our mom.

She eyed me. "So? For all I know, you're some weird third cousin making a money grab. Newsflash: the money's long gone."

"What money? Never mind—it doesn't matter. That's not why I'm here." I desperately wanted to tell her I was her sister and I loved her, but it would be too much. "Did you ever go to Afghanistan? Did you work for Doctors Without Borders?"

"Afghanistan?" She pulled her robe tighter, which only highlighted how frail she was. "What are you talking about?"

"You always wanted to be a doctor, right?" I could still remember waving goodbye to her at the airport when she flew to New Haven for medical school. She was crying— we'd never lived in separate states before—but beneath her tears, she was so brave, so determined. I'd felt then that every choice I'd made had been worth it, because her dreams were about to come true.

Now her bottom lip was quivering, just like it always did when she was on the verge of tears. "That wasn't in the cards for me."

Chris sneered. "Yeah, because hospitals usually frown on day drinking."

She spun around and glared at him. "Don't be a jerk, Chris."

I looked back and forth between them.

"He is a jerk. Also, you need to keep an eye on him. He's going to cheat on you with someone. Probably Lacy, though who knows."

"Hey, you're in my house right now. Watch what you say."

"I'm going to go now. Hattie, think about what I said."

Hattie looked at me with a mix of sadness and confusion. "I think you'd better leave."

***

I stood on the sidewalk and cried a little. I'd always thought that Christmas Eve couldn't get any worse. If only I'd known!

The sole silver lining—if you could even call it that—was that at least my parents weren't alive to see how everything had fallen apart.

The kids, I thought suddenly. I needed to go check on Chet, Dee Dee, and Jane.

Tony's house had dingy white siding before; now it was painted brick red, and there was a wreath hanging on the door. I felt my spirits begin to rise. If one good thing came out of this, it would be that Tony had finally gotten his act together and become the father his children deserved.

I knocked tentatively, wondering if Chris and Hattie were watching me or had called Tony to warn him. A few seconds later, a woman flung the door open. If I had to guess, I'd say she was in her mid-fifties. My stomach immediately sank; Tony wasn't there, and neither were the kids. Still, I had to ask.

"Does Tony Crawford live here?"

"I bought the house from him five years ago."

"I see. Do you happen to know where he and his kids went?"

She looked down at her slippers. "Those poor children."

"What do you mean?"

The woman leaned in to whisper. "Well, their mother ran off, and Tony's in jail. They're in foster care."

"With Reggie Nichols?" The longtime cannery employee was a great foster parent. Maybe the kids had lucked out.

"Reggie? I knew him, but he left town years ago."
Then she shuddered. "They're with another woman, and
she's no Reggie Nichols. I don't know if you know their
uncle, but it's hard for me to believe he didn't step in and
take them after his brother got locked up. I asked his wife,
Harriet, about it one time. She said he's just not cut out for
parenting. But I get the impression that's true for her, too.
I'm not one to talk, but she always smells like she spent the
night at Clarence's."

I felt like I'd just swallowed a boulder. "Thank you—
that's really helpful. Do you happen to know where the kids
are living now?"

"I'm not sure if I'm supposed to say, but you know the
little house over by the railroad?"

I couldn't even conceal my horror. "The shack with
the crooked roof? That looks like it could be blown away
with one strong gust of wind?"

She nodded. "That's where they live now. God bless
them, every one."

SEVEN

I fought waves of nausea as I headed toward the railroad tracks on the far end of town. Call it a sixth sense, but I knew that seeing my nieces and nephew would be the worst blow of the day, a fear that was confirmed when I heard crying from a quarter mile away. When I got closer to the shack, I saw Jane standing in the snow, screaming her head off.

"Jane? Are you okay?" I stood a few feet from her.

"Get away from me!" she growled. Her hair was matted beneath her hat, which was full of moth holes; her jacket was at least two sizes too small for her seven-year-old frame.

"You tell 'er, Janie." Chet was sitting on an old lawn chair in the middle of a yard that was strewn with scrap metal and broken bike parts. The shell of an old car, which looked it had been there for decades, had been discarded right next to the railroad tracks. He was filthy, too, and he was smoking. Thirteen and puffing away like a chimney! I had to force myself to look him in the eye.

"Why is she crying like that?"

He shrugged. "Keeps her warm? We've been out here for a good long time. The foster lady doesn't like us in the house before bedtime."

"But it's twelve degrees out."

He glanced at the shack. "Tell that to her."

Suddenly DeeDee came stumbling out the door. One of her cheeks was bright red.

I stared at her, aghast. "Did your foster parent hit you?"

"What's new?" Her voice was full of the righteous anger of a preteen, but her eyes were brimming with tears. "I hate her. You guys keep saying you'll move us, but nothing ever happens."

I realized then that the kids were the only people I'd encountered who hadn't asked me who I was. "What do you mean, 'you guys'?"

"You're with child protective services, right?"

I shook my head. "No, I'm one of your relatives."

"Great." Her voice was dripping with sarcasm. "We don't want your stupid promises. They literally never happen."

"I understand." Except I didn't, actually. "Does your uncle Chris ever help you?

"Uncle Chris? Yeah right. He doesn't care about anything or anyone. But especially not us."

Chet flicked his cigarette butt into the snow. "I'm getting a job next year and getting us out of here before that old witch breaks one of our bones or . . ." His voice trailed off.

"Or what, Chet?"

He winced, like I'd just hit him, too. "Worse, okay? Something worse."

I felt sick to my stomach. "Listen, I know you don't know me, but I'm going to fix this."

Jane peered up at me with big eyes. "How?"

"I don't know, but I'll figure it out. Now come on," I said. "Let's get out of here."

Chet shook his head. "We can't just leave."

"You said that she didn't want you inside until

dark, right?"

All three of them nodded.

"Good. So you've got hours before she even starts to notice you're gone. Don't worry. I'll make sure you get back in time."

I marched them back across town, to Chris and Hattie's. When they opened the door, they didn't look surprised to see me again. Then they spotted the kids standing behind me.

Chris's mouth fell open. "What in the Sam Hill?"

"As you're well aware, these are your nieces and nephew. They're living with an abusive foster parent who leaves them outside in the freezing cold and smacks them around." All of my years of running the cannery had taught me to take charge when the occasion called for it, but I was still surprised by how authoritative I sounded. "Now you and Hattie are going to give them a good, warm meal. Then you're going to get them some clothes that fit and keep them warm. Then you're going to feed them again, and when you take them back later, Chris, you are going to let that foster parent know that if anything happens to them before you sign the papers to become their new foster parent, you will personally show up to deal with it. You got it?"

"Why should I listen to you?" He looked fierce, but I knew him well enough to detect the hint of fear in his voice.

"Because it's Christmas Eve, and while you've made plenty of bad choices, you're not actually a bad person." I met Hattie's eye. "Today is hard, I know. But that's even more reason to take care of your parents' grandchildren, isn't it?"

"Okay." Hattie spoke without looking at Chris. "We'll do it."

He grunted in agreement.

"Great." I looked at the kids. "You guys going to be okay?"

The girls nodded solemnly.

Chet seemed less certain. "I guess."

I touched his shoulder lightly. "Believe me when I say I know exactly how hard it is to take care of your siblings after your parents are gone. But you're not just doing this for them." My voice caught, and I had to take a moment to collect myself. I looked over at Hattie, who had no idea that I was her sister. "You're doing it for you, too. You'll understand one day."

He nodded. "Hey. What's your name?"

"Bailey." I started for the door, then turned back. "Bailey George."

***

I started to cry as I walked down the stairs; by the time I was on the street, I was silently sobbing. Finally I understood how wonderful my life had been before. Had everything been perfect? Far from it. But although I didn't have Lacy or Chris anymore, I had a whole lot of people who loved me whom I loved, too.

There were Jessalyn and the countless other employees at the cannery. Even if I'd ultimately failed them, I'd provided them with eighteen years of solid work at a place where they were valued. That was not nothing.

Then there was my aunt Billie. Maybe I'd given her too much leeway. Then again, maybe what had happened had just been a dumb (if expensive) mistake. Either way,

I had needed her at my side all those years, weighing in on when to buy new equipment or whether it was time to promote or demote someone. And after she turned up behind the bar at Clarence's, void of all the warmth and humor that made her—well, her—it was hard not to make the case that she'd needed me just as much.

And of course, Hattie. She'd always gone out of her way to thank me for the sacrifices I'd made for her—and I'd always told her it was nothing. I shouldn't have. How many lives had she saved or touched because she had followed her dream of becoming a doctor? And I had helped make that happen. If that was my only purpose in this world, it was a darn good one.

I wiped my eyes on the sleeve of my coat, thinking of Chet, DeeDee, and Jane. Maybe I couldn't have children of my own—but that didn't mean I didn't have children in my life. It would be too easy for me to discount the role I'd played as their aunt. Now I understood that showing up every day, even if it was just to ask them about how school was going or to drop off some food, had made a difference in ways I never could have imagined.

I had to get back.

But how?

Maybe my brain was as frostbitten as my fingers were, because I headed to Clarence's without thinking about it. But as I got closer, I realized it was exactly where I wanted to be. After all, the bar was where I'd gotten myself into this mess.

Now there were at least a dozen people inside drinking away the bah-humbugs. I took a stool at the far end of the bar. My aunt Billie was nowhere to be seen, but a man was serving drinks. When he turned, I almost fell right off my stool.

"Nate? Is that you?" He was heavier than the night before, and his nose looked like it had been broken in two places, but I would have recognized him anywhere.

"Yeah, I'm Nate. Can I help you?" His voice was nasal, which made me wonder whether his nose job hadn't only been for cosmetic purposes.

I'd long since figured out that no one else could recognize me, but it was a shock to see him treat me like a stranger.

As he stared at me, it came rushing back. I did remember Nate from high school. More specifically, I remembered Tony, Chris, and a couple of their other friends cornering Nate in the hallway one day. I'd pushed my way through them and told them to find a better way to spend their time. Maybe because Chris and I had just started dating, they'd actually listened to me and left him alone. That was why he recognized me the night before.

I blinked several times, clearing the image from my mind. "I'd like a whiskey—neat, please."

"Sure thing." He nodded and, less than a minute later, slid the drink toward me. "You visiting for the holidays?"

"Something like that. Hey, have you ever been to L.A.? I hear it's nice, especially this time of year."

He got a faraway look in his eyes. "Funny you say that—I've always wanted to live there, at least for a while. I used to think I'd start a distillery out there, make my own gin." He shrugged. "I guess pouring it instead of making it isn't the worst thing."

It wasn't—but I couldn't get over how all of the sparkle I'd seen in him the night before was missing. "Did you ever try to head out west?"

"Nah."

"Why not?"

He shrugged and looked toward the bar for a moment. "Sometimes one small thing leads to another, and before you know it your whole life turned out nothing like you thought it would. Know what I mean?"

Did I ever. "Definitely. But it's not too late to make a change, is it?"

"I don't know. Maybe it is, and maybe it isn't. What about you? Now that you know what I wish I'd done with my life, got any secret wishes of your own?"

"Oh, me?" I took a long swig of my whiskey, relishing the burning sensation in my throat. Then I looked him straight in the eye. "I wish I'd been born."

EIGHT

My head felt like it was being hammered by a hundred tiny elves. And who had shoved cotton balls in my mouth while I was asleep? Everything hurt so much that I had to be coming down with a bug.

I sat straight up.

I wasn't sick—I was hungover! And I was back in Nate's loft, where boxes were strewn everywhere and my cell phone was on top of my coat, just as I'd left it before I'd woken up in a world in which I'd never existed.

Had anything so wonderful ever happened?

"Hello?" I yelled as I rose from the sofa. If Nate was here—and I was praying to God that he was, because that would officially make all of this real—I wanted to know.

"Morning." He called to me from the kitchen. I stared at him for a moment, making sure I wasn't imagining him. He was rubbing his eyes, and sure enough, his old new nose was back, and he was in plaid flannel pajamas, looking as lean as a pro soccer player. "I was just putting coffee on. I see that you're feeling better?"

"I am!" I grinned, even though I needed a toothbrush like a shark needs water. "But I had the strangest dream!"

"Oh, yeah?"

I nodded. "It was—well, the whole thing is too complicated to explain. But just before I woke up, I dreamed that you told me you'd always wanted to open a distillery, but instead of going out to L.A. to do that, you ended up being a bartender at Clarence's."

His face went all funny. "Did you Google me?"

"No." It occurred to me that maybe I should have before agreeing to spend the night at his apartment. "Why?"

"How about some coffee, and then I'll explain?"

"That sounds amazing."

He handed me a steaming mug and the cream. Then I sat across from him at his kitchen island and waited.

"So, here's the thing, Bailey. I don't want to freak you out—"

"You do know when you say that, I'm going to be

freaked out, right?"

He laughed. "Fair enough. Point being, I do run a distillery back in California."

My mouth fell open. "You do?"

He smiled shyly. "Yeah, and it turns out I'm pretty good at it. I'm actually looking to expand—that's another reason I'm here. I know this community could use a serious cash infusion."

"That's an understatement."

"So . . . I saw your ad in the paper. I was going to reach out next week about touring the cannery. I think it would be the perfect place to set up operations."

"Please don't joke."

He frowned, but there was a twinkle in his eye. "I would never. But it's a little complicated."

"How so?" Just then, my phone rang on the other side of the room. "I'm sorry—I have to get that because it's probably my sister. I'm supposed to pick her up from the train station in a little while." I slapped my forehead. "My car is at Clarence's. What are the odds he's open at eight a.m. on Christmas Eve?"

"Slim to none. But I'll take you over to the station."

"Really?"

He nodded. "Go answer the phone. I'll find you a toothbrush."

I smiled at him. "You really are the best."

"Bet you say that to all the guys."

I thought of Chris—*real* Chris, but also the angry guy in my dream, or whatever that alternate reality had been—and shook my head. "Nope. Just you."

He grinned. "For that, I'll drive you anywhere you want to go."

On the way to the train station, I peered out the window of Nate's truck. All the gray was gone; everything was glittering and white. I thought that it was quite possibly the most beautiful sight I had ever seen, until I saw Hattie waiting outside the train station.

Nate had barely stopped his truck when I jumped out and ran to her. I threw my arms around her and hugged her tight. "You're not too skinny and you don't smell like booze! And you're finally here!"

She pulled back and laughed. "Were you expecting

something else?"

"Let's just say I had a very bad dream last night."

"Well, it's over now."

"And thank heaven for that." I looped my arm through hers. "Come on. I have so much to tell you."

***

Hattie and I needed to make a hotel reservation, but first, Nate offered to make us brunch. When we pulled up to his apartment building, Lacy was waiting on the steps. Her eyes were red and she looked like she hadn't slept. "Bailey. Please, can we talk?"

I glanced at Hattie and Nate. "Can you guys give me a minute?"

I'd told Hattie about the affair on the car ride over. Now she glared at Lacy. "I don't want to leave you alone with her."

I couldn't help but smile at my younger sister, being protective of me. "I'll be fine, Hattie. She weighs ninety pounds soaking wet."

Lacy sniffed. "A hundred."

"Exactly."

Nate put his hand on my arm and smiled softly. "Just hit the intercom or call if you need anything, okay?"

He was looking at me intently, and my stomach did a little flip. "I will."

Lacy started to cry before they disappeared inside. "Oh, Bailey! I'm an idiot!"

"Maybe." I sighed. "But mostly I don't get it, Lacy. I just don't understand why you threw away three decades of friendship. Chris isn't even that great in bed."

That got a tiny laugh out of her. But then she started crying again—a terrible hacking that sounded like she was on the verge of hyperventilating. "It's just that—I ruined— Christmas—for you!"

"You didn't ruin Christmas for me. Nothing can do that." As I heard myself say this, I realized that it was true. Not Lacy and Chris. Not Billie's mistake. Not even my parents' death.

She sniffled. "Are you still going to have the Christmas party?"

I shook my head. "I haven't cancelled it yet, but I

probably should."

"What do you mean?"

"The cannery's in trouble, Lacy. I'm going to have to close it down."

Her eyes grew wide. "How bad is it?"

"Bad." I considered telling her the whole story, but she'd hear it around town soon enough. "We're two hundred thousand under water."

She staggered backward. "Whoa. That's a lot of money. I wish I had that kind of cash lying around. I'd give it to you."

Yes, it was a lot of money. But then I realized that I knew someone who had that kind of cash. Someone who owed me, big time.

"Listen, I've got to get going. I'm going to miss you, Lacy."

Her cheeks were wet and streaked with mascara. "I know you'll never forgive me, Bailey."

I smiled sadly. "Forgive? Sure, I will—I am my mother's daughter, after all. Forget? Not a chance."

She wiped her nose on her sleeve. "I deserve that."

She deserved much more, but I wasn't going to be the one to give it to her. As terrible as I felt about the way she and Chris had betrayed me, I wasn't the one who had to live with the knowledge that I'd ruined not one but two great relationships because I couldn't keep my pants on.

She was crying again. "This doesn't have to be goodbye, Bae. Please, can we be friends?"

Some mistakes in life were unfixable, and this was one of them. Lacy would learn that soon enough. For now, I stepped forward and hugged her, which surprised her. I wished her a Merry Christmas.

Then I went to see about doing something about the things that could still be fixed.

NINE

In light of all that had just transpired, I decided the Christmas party was still on—and that it would take place at our house, just like every year. After all, that's what my parents would have wanted.

But first, I needed to talk to Chris about a few things. Including but not limited to the fact that I was going to need our house back.

I didn't intend to stay there for long, and I sure wasn't going anywhere near the bedroom. But Hattie needed a place to sleep, and so did I. So I asked Nate if he would drive us back to the bungalow.

As we made our way to the other side of town, I couldn't help but think about the last Christmas I spent with my parents—which happened to be the first I spent with Chris. We'd started dating my senior year of high school, but he dumped me shortly after prom, saying he wasn't ready to get serious. I was crushed. My ever-wise mom, however, told me not to let on that it bothered me. Either he'd come around or I'd find someone better, she said.

Sure enough: by the first week of October of my freshman year of college, Chris showed up outside my dorm with daisies—my favorite—and a plea for me to forgive him and take him back. By the time Thanksgiving rolled around, we'd exchanged those three little words and started talking about our future together.

That Christmas, my mom hung a stocking for him, and he showed up just as she was serving pancakes and bacon. After breakfast, we checked our stockings. Every year, my father bought a gag gift for my mom—a toilet-shaped mug one time, coal candy another, and once a fancy-looking jewelry box that contained a candy ring that my mom wore the rest of the day. Hattie and I got in on the fun at some point, and targeted each other. One year I hung her stocking from a hook on the ceiling; another, she filled mine with peeled grapes. Naturally, I thought the best way to welcome Chris into our family was to prank him, too.

I glued wrapping paper to a box of cereal and put it beneath the tree for him.

I'd bit my lip as I watched him try to unwrap his present. I kept waiting for him to realize it was a joke, but his face grew redder and redder as he tried to pull the paper away.

My mom had to break it to him. "It's a joke, Chris. It's our family tradition."

Instead of laughing, he'd stormed out of the living room, as angry as a bag full of hornets.

The following day, my mom casually mentioned the incident. "You're sure about Chris?"

I assured her I was.

"Does he laugh easily in other situations?" This was the closest she'd ever come to criticizing him.

I'd nodded. "He'll get used to our weird rituals."

Of course, I'd missed her point. But now I got it. It wasn't about him getting used to anything. It was about how seriously he took himself. The way he took everything, really. My mom—the woman who sought out the best in everyone—had spotted something in him that gave her pause.

I wished I'd listened. Maybe if my mom had lived, she'd have had more chances to warn me before he and I stood before a minister and fifty of our nearest and dearest and vowed to love each other for the rest of our natural lives.

For the very first time, I realized that maybe it was for the best that we hadn't been able to have kids together.

We pulled up to the house, and Nate looked at me with concern. "You sure about this?"

Hattie piped up from the back seat. "You don't have to do this, you know."

I shook my head. "Actually, I do."

Chris's eyes were red and swollen when he answered the door. I couldn't tell if he was hungover or had been crying. Maybe both. For a split second, I wanted to comfort him and ask how I could make it better. Then I felt kind of sick because I would never be able to do that again.

I remembered what my aunt Billie had said to me after my parents died. "Their death can't change all the good times you had with them, Bailey. It took their lives, but it can't take the memories you have of them."

It was still true. Likewise, Chris's betrayal stole the future we would have had together. But it couldn't erase my good memories, and there was something comforting in that.

"Bailey. Um, hi. I'm—"

I held up a hand to stop him. "Don't. I know you're sorry, and I don't think you have any idea how sorry you're going to be once it sinks in that you just lost the best thing that ever happened to you."

"I already know that."

"Good. But I'm here to talk to you about something else. I need a loan."

The hope that had flitted across his face was gone just as fast. "What?"

"My aunt Billie lost some money, and I need it to make payroll for the cannery. Otherwise I'm not going to be able to pay everyone in two days—or ever again, most likely. That includes your brother." I stole a glance at Tony's house. "I think we both know how much he needs that job."

Chris looked nervous. "How much money are we talking?"

"Two hundred."

He reached into his pants for his wallet.

"Grand, Chris. I need two hundred grand."

He balked. "That's almost everything I've got."

"It's not, actually." I'd seen his bank statements. "And I'm not asking you to give it to me for good. I'm asking for a loan. Let's say two years, no interest. I think it's the least you can do."

"Bailey . . ."

"Listen, Chris. I've never asked you for anything. All these years, you've sat around and moped and I never even asked you to do the dishes. Granted, that's partially my fault, but you were more than happy to watch me go work my butt off all day, then take care of almost everything else in our lives. And for that privilege, you rewarded me by sleeping with my best friend." I wrinkled my nose. "That's really gross. You could have picked literally anyone else and it would have been better than Lacy." I almost added that she didn't love him, but for all I knew, she did. I didn't care.

"I'm sorry, Bailey." He looked so pathetic, so downtrodden, that I knew he really meant it. I was glad he was at least remorseful.

"Bank's open 'til noon—better get your shoes on. Oh, and Chris?"

His right eye was twitching the way it always did when he was nervous. Good. "Yeah?"

"I'm going to need you to move in with Lacy as soon as we get back from the bank. We're going to sell the house sooner rather than later, but for now, Hattie and I need a place to stay." I smiled sweetly at him. "You're welcome to come to the party tonight, of course—but don't even think about spending the night."

TEN

"How are you holding up, Bailey? I can't believe everything you've been through in the past few days."

Hattie and I were standing in my kitchen, making cookies for the party. It was nice. Normal, even. If I didn't think too much, I could almost forget about Chris and Lacy. But at least the cannery would stay open. Just knowing that my employees would be paid on time—for this paycheck and many more—was enough to put me in a festive mood.

"I'm better than I should be." I considered telling her about the dream for a split second, then decided against it. It wouldn't make sense, and anyway, what was most important was what I did as a result of it.

"I'm relieved to hear that. So . . ." Out of the corner of my eye, I could see she was grinning at me. "Nate seems nice."

"He is." I smiled to myself, thinking about the hug he'd given me after he dropped me and Hattie off. "I like him."

Hattie bumped her hip against mine. "Oh, I can tell."

I laughed. "Can I just say how happy I am to have you home?"

"I'm happy to be home. I just wish I'd been able to make it earlier."

"You're here now. That's all that matters."

She nodded and put the baking sheet in the oven. "Do you want to go see Mom and Dad tomorrow?"

"At the cemetery?" I usually took Chris with me when I went to visit their gravestones, but it had been at least half a year since I'd last been.

"It doesn't have to be tomorrow. I know it's Christmas and all."

"No, tomorrow's good."

Hattie hoisted herself up on the counter. "Great, because I don't want to go without you."

I wiped down the counter, then hopped up beside her and put my arm around her. "Me neither. Now tell me everything about your life abroad and all the lives you've been saving."

***

Six hours later, the doorbell started to ring. First Jessalyn arrived with Jamar, her boyfriend. Like last year, they were both dressed in funny Christmas sweaters.

I threw my arms around her. "You don't know how happy I am to see you."

"Child, I saw you just yesterday." Her warm brown eyes crinkled at the corners. "But I'll take it."

I smiled at her. "Get used to it, because I am going to be telling you how much I appreciate you a lot more often from here on out."

She laughed. "I won't say no to that."

Next Tony and the kids showed up. "Hi, Bailey." Tony seemed almost bashful as he greeted me. "Thanks for having us. Given, uh. You know. The situation."

"Yep, I know." I put my hand on his shoulder. "But you and the kids are my family. That's not going to change. Speaking of!" I knelt down and Jane, wearing a fluffy red dress, came running into my arms.

"Aunt Bailey!"

"Hiya, kiddo." I ruffled her hair and oh man—here came the waterworks again. I blinked furiously. "You look like a million bucks."

"You, too." She squeezed me.

"Thank you." I stood and put my arms out to Chet and DeeDee. "You guys. I love you so much, and I am always—always—here for you. No matter what. You know that, right?"

Chet was blushing under his freckles, but DeeDee wrapped her arm around my waist. "We know."

I squeezed her. "Good."

"Bailey?" My aunt had just poked her head out of the kitchen.

"Aunt Billie!" I motioned for her to come over, then slung an arm around her neck. "You're here! I thought I'd see you at Clarence's the other night, but you were already gone."

She was staring at me incredulously. "You're not mad at me? I thought for sure once it sunk in . . ."

"Mad? No. It's just money."

She looked mournful. "It's a lot of money."

"Yes, it is, but safe to say you'll never drain the company account again. And I have good news: Chris loaned me enough to cover payroll."

"He did?"

I nodded. Chris hadn't been happy about it, but he'd still driven me over to the bank to make the transfer. "Even better, I have a great lead on a distillery that wants to set up shop in half of the cannery."

"Oh, Bailey!" Billie looked a decade younger than she had not a minute earlier. "That's wonderful."

"Yes, it is."

More than a dozen people streamed in—neighbors, friends, cannery employees who were family now. As I looked around, it struck me that every single one of them *was* a gift.

Hattie was making the rounds, passing out eggnog and champagne. When she reached me, I took the tray and set it on the coffee table. Then I handed her a glass of champagne and took one for myself.

I pinged the side of my glass with a fork until the room grew quiet. "I'd like to make a toast! To my sister, Hattie, who flew all the way from Afghanistan to be with us tonight."

She smiled at me. "Thank you. I'm so happy to be here! But I'd like to make a toast, too." She lifted her champagne flute. "To my sister, who's my hero. I wouldn't have become a doctor if it weren't for her. Heck, I wouldn't have made it this far in life if it weren't for her. To Bailey!"

"To Bailey!" Everyone lifted their glasses to me, and I beamed at them through my tears. How lucky I was; how blessed.

Then I heard another bell ring, and in marched Clarence, with Nate right behind him.

Nate weaved through the crowd until he reached me. I smiled shyly at him. "Thanks for picking up Clarence."

He winked. "Of course. Neither of us would have missed this for the world."

He was wearing a dark green sweater over a red plaid shirt and hadn't shaved off his stubble. He looked entirely too good. "Hey, when we were talking about the distillery earlier, you mentioned that it was complicated. How so?"

"Oh. That."

My face fell. He was going to tell me that it wasn't going to work. I would find a way to pay Chris back and get the cannery in good standing. But the solution wouldn't involve Nate.

But then he grinned and put his arms around my waist. "Well, the thing is, Bailey George, I do want to go into business with you. In fact, I've been sure about that this entire time. But there might be a conflict of interest."

"Oh yeah?" I smiled out of relief, but also because I liked the feel of his body against mine. "What's that?"

He grinned. "I've been crazy about you since I set eyes on you in tenth grade, and, well—I was kind of hoping, since you're newly if unexpectedly single, we might go on a date or twenty."

I laughed. "I think I'd be willing to mix business and pleasure this one time."

"I was hoping you'd say that." Now he was pulling me across the room. Before I could ask him where we were going, we stopped in the hallway near the front door. And above our heads was a sprig of mistletoe that someone at the party must have hung.

My heart was fluttering in my chest, but it was a good feeling, one I hadn't had in a long time. Nate's arms felt strong and right around me, and the way he was looking at me told me that whatever happened next, this man would not break my heart. "Merry Christmas, Nate."

"Merry Christmas, Bailey." Then he pulled me closer and kissed me.

I let myself melt into him. I was no longer a wonderful wife. But to be here, among the people I loved, made this a wonderful life—one I would never take for granted again.

AUTHOR'S NOTE

If you enjoyed *It's a Wonderful Wife*, please take a second to write a brief review; reviews make a world of difference in a book's success.

If you already did, thank you! Either way, thank you for taking the time to read my latest. You, dear reader, are why I write.

ABOUT THE AUTHOR

Camille Pagán writes about love, relationships, and making the most of this wonderfully messy life. She's the #1 Amazon Charts and *Washington Post* bestselling author of eight novels, including *I'm Fine and Neither Are You*, *Woman Last Seen in Her Thirties*, and *Life and Other Near-Death Experiences*, which has been optioned for film. Her work has also been published in *The New York Times*, *O: The Oprah Magazine*, *Real Simple*, *Time*, and many others.

When Camille's not writing her next story, you'll usually find her with her family, talking shop with other writers, or at the beach—with a book in hand, of course. Sign up for her newsletter to be the first to hear about her new novels, giveaways, and updates at CamillePagan.com/subscribe.